BEFORE THE SUNSET ENDS

TWO BOYS, ONE TRUTH, AND THE SEA BETWEEN

VIVEK MOHAN

To Shahir —
For being my muse, my mirror, and my motivation.
Your love for stories, your unwavering support, and your
belief in me gave this book its first breath.
This is as much yours as it is mine.

Contents

Acknowledgements

This story would not have come to life without the unwavering support and inspiration of a few incredible people.

To Shahir, my partner — thank you for being the spark that pushed me to put pen to paper. Your creativity, encouragement, and belief in me have been my greatest motivators throughout this journey.

To Anjna, my dear friend — your constant push and belief in this story gave me the courage to take the leap and share it with the world. Thank you for seeing the value in my words even when I doubted them.

To Nisha, my ex-wife and dear friend—thank you for your unconditional support and kindness. Your acceptance and encouragement during my exploration of sexuality and gender meant more than words can say. You showed me that love can evolve, and that compassion is what truly binds us.

To everyone who believes in stories like Adam and Ishaan's — this is for you.

CHAPTER ONE

NOT ALL SUNDAYS SMELL LIKE SANDALWOOD

Adam Mathew had a complicated relationship with Sundays.

At twenty, life already felt like a never-ending slideshow of blurry mornings, awkward conversations, and existential questions that refused to come with subtitles. This particular Sunday was no different—except maybe a bit sadder than the others. And it had nothing to do with the leftover appam in the fridge or the fact that his favorite t-shirt had shrunk in the wash (again). No. It was something deeper. Something that clung to his chest like a damp shirt in monsoon.

The waves of Puthenthodu beach stretched lazily before him, dragging and retreating like an old auntie's gossip. Adam sat on a crumbling concrete slab near the beach, knees pulled close to his chest, staring into the salty blur of the Arabian Sea. His straight black hair stuck to his forehead, the breeze doing little to lift it. He looked like a painting someone had given up on midway—pale, average build, mostly unfinished.

Around him, a few boys laughed and posed for selfies, their joy so loud it scratched his ears. Adam squinted at them. Not in judgment. Just... envy, maybe. Or confusion. How were they so sure of themselves? Why did they seem to have it figured out while he was stuck watching life like a dull Instagram story you can't skip?

He had skipped church this morning. Again.
Not out of rebellion. Just... exhaustion. From pretending. From smiling during the Peace be with yous and pretending to care about St. Paul's letter to the Corinthians when all he really wanted was someone to write him a letter.

He sighed, stood up, brushed the sand off his pants like it was a bad mood, and got on his cycle.

By the time Adam reached home, the Sunday sun had begun turning everything sweaty. His house—a charmingly disoriented mix of Portuguese tiles and Malayali chaos—stood like a memory refusing to move on.

"Da, where were you?" boomed his father, Matthew Tharakan, as soon as Adam pushed open the creaky gate. A stout man with a thick moustache and a Bible always within arm's reach, Matthew was more punctual about mass than the parish priest.

"I just needed some air," Adam muttered, parking the cycle.

"You needed Jesus. Not air! Church is not a drive-thru, Adam!"

"Chettai..." began his mother, Lissy Tharakan, crying out from the dining room, gently placing a bowl of kadala curry on the table. She was petite but strong-willed, like tea with extra ginger.

"Let him be. He's probably tired from strolling."

Adam shot her a grateful look. She always knew when to step in and when to not ask too many questions. It was her superpower.

"Hi Chetta!" chirped a voice from the stairs. His younger sister, Aleena, a precocious 16-year-old with a TikTok addiction and a dramatic flair that deserved its own reality show, peeped down, holding her phone, which has become a part of herself. He smiled faintly. "Morning, drama queen."

Adam half-heartedly dipped a piece of appam into the curry and chewed like he was being punished. Appa continued to lecture between spoonfuls of breakfast, Lissy tactfully changed the subject to Aleena's school play, and Adam? He just wanted to disappear into a puff of coastal mist.

Without finishing his food, he mumbled something about a headache and stomped off to his room.

The second the door clicked shut, the real Adam returned.

He lay flat on his bed, arms sprawled, staring at the ceiling like it held answers in Morse code. The fan spun above—lazy, like his ambition. His chest felt like a balloon that forgot how to float. There was a weight that couldn't be seen, only felt, right between his ribs.

Was he lonely? Probably.

Was he confused? Definitely.

Was he dramatic about it? Well, yes—but only in private.

After rolling around for a bit like a burrito of melancholy, he reached for his sketchbook. It was hidden under a stack of untouched college notes and a dusty guitar he kept for aesthetic purposes.

On the page from last night, a half-finished sketch stared back at him. Two silhouettes—facing each other, but not touching. A heart between them, melting into the horizon like a sunset.

He traced the lines with his fingers and sighed.

Maybe next Sunday would feel a little less heavy.

Maybe the silence in his chest would stop echoing so loud.

He closed the sketchbook, placed it beside him, and curled up like a question mark. There were no answers today. Just the familiar ache of wanting something more—something he couldn't quite name.

But at least, for now, the sea had listened.

CHAPTER TWO

ALGORITHMS AND ALMOSTS

A few days earlier...

At Acquinas College of Science & Humanities, Wednesdays were a paradox. They carried mid-week lethargy but came loaded with double lab hours, a rotating canteen menu, and the persistent smell of wet socks from the boys' locker room.

Adam Mathew sat in the third row of the B.Sc. Computer Science class, staring blankly at a screen full of code he had already solved ten minutes ago. His chin rested on his palm, eyes half-open, looking like an undercooked pancake with zero toppings.

"Adam," the professor called out, "Done already?"

He nodded without looking up. "Yeah, sir."

"You could help your classmates then."

He nodded again. Didn't move. Just clicked on the minimize button and opened his drawing app for a quick scribble of a half-eaten sandwich with wings. It was oddly satisfying.

Adam liked coding—he genuinely did. The problem-solving, the logic, the clean satisfaction of getting a program right. It was the only thing, besides drawing, that made him feel a little less fuzzy in the head. But once he finished his tasks, the silence would crawl back in, tapping at his shoulder like an old classmate you're trying to avoid.

His world at college was a tiny constellation of three friends.

There was Freddy—real name Friedrich—a lanky boy with curly hair and the soul of a stand-up comic who hadn't yet made peace with his GPA.

Then Mabin, the campus cricket star who claimed he could reverse swing even an eraser if given a chance.

And finally, Vaishnavi—sharp, sarcastic, and the one person who felt closest to Adam without needing a reason.

When the bell rang for lunch, the trio scooped up their bags and headed out into the shaded courtyard, dodging the canteen stampede like pros. Vaishnavi caught up with them, waving a dramatic goodbye to her girl gang like a soap opera heroine about to board a train.

"Adam, can you show me the logic for the palindrome function?" she asked, tossing her duffel bag on the bench beside him. "I swear I tried. The only thing I could successfully reverse was my patience."

Adam smirked and nodded. "You missed a semicolon. That's it."

"I knew it. My enemies shall face consequences," she declared, pulling out her lunch box like it was a mic drop.

Mabin and Freddy laughed. The air felt light for a moment, interrupted only when Vaishnavi leaned in a little too close to Adam, brushing her shoulder against his. He shifted slightly, an almost-invisible reflex. She didn't seem to notice—or maybe she did and chose not to mention it.

"You coming for the cricket trials?" she asked, mouth half-full. "Mabin says they're shortlisting for the college tournament today."

Freddy raised an eyebrow. "You play?"

"I mean, yeah," Adam muttered. "Used to."

"Bro, this is your chance to un-snooze your college life," Mabin grinned. "Do it for the team. Also, I need someone to fetch water when I become captain."

The sun was just beginning to dip when Adam stood near the dusty cricket pitch, pads strapped clumsily to his legs, helmet in hand, squinting through the glare. Mabin was already on the field, showing off some textbook footwork that made the Physical Education teacher nod approvingly.

On the sidelines, a small group of girls cheered and clapped, Vaishnavi among them. She waved dramatically when she saw Adam. He waved back with a half-smile.

Then came the bowler.

Tall. Broad-shouldered. Dark complexion with a jawline that looked like it was carved by the gods of Malayalam cinema. His jersey bore the name Rahil, and Adam had seen him around before. Always laughing with seniors. Always confident. Always... kind of unsettling.

And now, Rahil stood a few feet away, cracking his knuckles with the focus of a man about to prove a point.

Adam gripped the bat tighter.

Don't mess this up, Adam.

First ball. He connected, barely. A lazy drive.

Second ball—missed. His head wasn't following the line.

Third—edge.

Fourth—decent pull shot.

Fifth—complete miss.

Sixth—drive into mid-off, but the timing was off.

He stepped off the pitch, disappointed. His shirt clung to his back. The weight of all the "almosts" pressed down on his shoulders.

Rahil laughed with the other seniors. Not mockingly, but still—it stung.

Adam looked up, their eyes met for a fraction of a second. Rahil smirked. Just a little.

And Adam hated how his stomach flipped.

Mabin jogged up to him, panting, a grin spread across his sweat-slicked face. "Man, you did okay! They might still shortlist you."

Adam didn't respond. Just handed over the bat and walked past him, deflated.

Vaishnavi appeared next to him, water bottle in hand, her expression soft. "Hey. Don't be so hard on yourself."

"I'm fine," he muttered, wiping his face with the edge of his shirt.

"You're allowed to have an off day, you know?" she said, gently.

Adam didn't answer. He just nodded, eyes focused on the fading pink sky over Acquinas.

That evening, back in his room, Adam couldn't stop replaying the look on Rahil's face.
The smirk.
The confidence.
The mystery of it all.

It lingered in his mind like the echo of a song you didn't want to remember but couldn't forget.

He stared at the ceiling, the fan spinning lazily above him, casting long, slow-moving shadows on the walls. The room was silent except for the soft hum of the city outside and the uneven rhythm of his breath.

But more than the memory of Rahil's face, he hated the strange ache it left behind.

It wasn't just sadness. It was more complicated.

A bruise of disappointment.

A sting of guilt.

A hollow kind of shame that sat quietly in his chest, saying nothing, but taking up all the space.

He turned to his side, curling up like he used to as a child after nightmares.

But this one, he knew, he couldn't wake up from.

He wasn't haunted by what happened.

He was haunted by what it meant.

Sunday Evenings and Serendipity

After a plate of spicy pazham pori and a glass of tea made sweeter than necessary by his mother—bless her soul—Adam hopped onto his old cycle, the one that squeaked a little every time he turned left.

This was routine.

Not the cycle squeaking—that was just a persistent problem.

But the beach. The beach was sacred.

Ever since school ended, Sunday evenings belonged to the sea. No friends. No assignments. No lectures about "godlessness" from his father. Just Adam and the waves.

He parked his cycle near the same coconut tree. The one that tilted ever-so-slightly to the left, like it, too, was tired of everything.

The beach was alive. The morning's solitude had given way to the evening's chaos—families spreading out like picnics, kids building sandcastles that looked more like sandlumps, vendors yelling over the sea breeze, and couples... so many couples.

Hand in hand. Leaning on each other. Laughing into each other's necks like the world wasn't falling apart.

Adam turned away from them all.

He walked down the sand to his spot. The rickety concrete slab from where the view was uninterrupted. Where the sound of the waves drowned out everything else. Where the ocean did what it always did—came close, then left. Came close, then left.Just like people.

Adam wrapped his arms around his knees and stared ahead. He let his mind drift. To the cricket tryouts. To the smirk on Rahil's face. To Vaishnavi's concerned voice. To his father's words that still clung to the back of his neck like a badly stitched collar.

"Skipping church doesn't mean you'll find peace, da."

But here he was. Trying.

The waves kept crashing gently. Rhythmically. Patiently.

And then—a football hit him.

Square in the side.

He jolted up with a startled "Ow!" and turned around, brushing sand off his shirt, expecting a bunch of noisy kids.

Instead, a boy ran toward him.

Shirtless. Athletic. Bronze-skinned with curly hair that bounced as he moved. Wearing only a pair of navy-blue shorts. His chest glistened with sweat under the fading golden light. He looked like he had just jogged out of a postcard from Goa.

"Sorry! Really sorry!" the boy called out as he slowed down, clearly out of breath. "Didn't mean to hit you."

His voice was surprisingly soft. Polite. Almost... careful.

Adam blinked. "It's okay. No damage done."

He could smell the salt, the sweat, the warm, sunbaked skin. His stomach felt weird again—like all the butterflies from earlier were still waiting for their turn to flutter.

Another boy from across the beach cupped his hands around his mouth and yelled, "He gets hit all the time! Don't worry! He's built for impact!"

Adam rolled his eyes. "Charming."

The boy next to him laughed—light and airy. "Ignore him. Church acquaintance. He thinks he's funny."

Adam chuckled despite himself.

"I'll get the ball and head back," the boy said, motioning toward where it had rolled. Then, almost like an afterthought, he turned back with a smile and said, "I'm Ishaan. New around here."

He offered a hand. Adam hesitated for a microsecond before shaking it.

"I'm Adam."

"Nice to meet you, Adam," Ishaan said, still smiling. "Sorry again. Hope I didn't ruin your quiet."

"Not really. Just gave me a reason to stretch," Adam replied.

Ishaan nodded, retrieved the ball, and jogged back to his group.

Adam watched him go, an odd warmth bubbling in his chest that didn't feel like just beach heat.

Something about him felt... different.

Unexplainable.

Like a glitch in the system that didn't need fixing.

Adam leaned back into his usual spot, arms folded behind his head, eyes on the darkening sky.
The ocean didn't feel as heavy now.
Not today.

There was still salt in the breeze... but now, mixed in with it, lingered something else—something warm and human. The faint trace of sweat and sunshine that clung to Ishaan's skin had somehow stayed with him, curling around his senses like a forgotten tune. It shouldn't have meant anything. But somehow, it did.

Adam peeked into the boys playing, finding Ishaan dribbling the ball with ease. And for reasons he couldn't fully explain, Adam closed his eyes—and smiled.

CHAPTER FOUR

The Sound of Sunday

The night had a quiet charm to it—the kind that wrapped itself around the Tharakan household and gently asked everyone to slow down.

Adam sat curled into the corner of the family couch, a plate of banana chips half-eaten on the table, as the TV played the familiar opening jingle of Voice of Kerala. It was a Sunday night ritual, unspoken but sacred. His younger sister, Aleena, sat cross-legged on the floor, fully immersed, pretending to be one of the judges. His mother, Lissy, chuckled every time Aleena hit the imaginary buzzer.

Adam smiled faintly. It was peaceful.

During a break, Appa cleared his throat and stood up. "Adam... just a minute, moné. Come with me."

Adam followed, unsure whether it was about church again. But the moment they stepped onto the veranda, the mood shifted. The air was crisp with a trace of jasmine from the neighbor's garden. The sky above was clear for once, a few stars daring to shine through.

Mathew Tharakan didn't speak immediately. He leaned on the railing, arms crossed, eyes on the road ahead the gates, like he was watching memories float by.

"You remember the time you fell into the pond behind Valyappachan's house?" he said, suddenly. "You were what—six? Thought you could catch a fish with your bare hands."

Adam let out a tiny laugh. "You jumped in after me before even kicking your shoes off."

Mathew smiled. "And Amma scolded both of us like mad."

There was a long pause. Then, his voice lowered.

"You were fearless back then, moné. And sensitive too. You used to cry if someone stepped on a snail. I loved that about you." He looked at Adam then, his voice now soft, steady. "I don't know what's going on in your head these days. I can sense... something. But whatever it is, I want you to know—you're not alone. You'll never be."

Adam blinked, caught off guard.

"Appacha," he began, but his throat tightened.

He stepped forward and wrapped his arms around his father, the hug tighter than he intended. And for a moment, Adam just held on—like he was six again, like the pond water was cold and the world too big.

Inside, Lissy and Aleena peeked through the curtain. Neither said a word, but their eyes shimmered with quiet pride.

Dinner that night was Lissy's iconic Sunday beef vindaloo—tangy, rich, the kind that lingered on your fingers and in your memory. They all gathered around the table, dipping flaky parottas into the thick gravy, talking over each other, laughing too loudly, and reaching for the last piece like it was the family tradition.

Later, Adam retreated to his room with a full belly and a full heart.

He dusted off his old guitar and sat by the window. The night outside was warm and quiet. Coconut trees swayed under a sleepy moon. Somewhere in the distance, he could hear murmurs from the neighbors—an argument about chutney, or maybe cricket.

He strummed a few rusty chords, letting his fingers remember what his mind had forgotten.

And then—uninvited but welcome—came a memory. A flash of bronze skin. Curly hair. That warm, sunlit scent.

Ishaan.

The strings went still.

Adam set the guitar aside, moved over to his bed and slowly pulled the sheets over him, and lay there in silence.

As he lay down, he squeezed his eyes shut.

And like that, Adam pushed the thought away.

CHAPTER FIVE

MISSION ACQUAINTANCE

Aquinas College was buzzing again. Monday morning sun filtered through the dusty windows of the third-floor classroom, where Adam sat half-slouched over his notebook, absentmindedly drawing little spirals in the corner of the last page.

His professor was talking about data structures, but Adam was deep in a different kind of loop.

He needed a lover.

Well, someone, at least. Someone to walk with during breaks. Someone to talk to without thinking twice. Someone who laughed at his sarcasm, who sat too close without thinking it was weird. Someone like what Freddy had.

Freddy, who sat three benches away, was smiling at his phone—again. Probably a text from Sharon. They were always texting. Always sitting next to each other during lunch. Always giggling over something that made the rest of them feel like mildly awkward extras in a rom-com.

Adam glanced at him, then sighed.

When was the last time I felt... happy-happy? School maybe. Those early days before everything got complicated. Before the voice in his head started whispering things he couldn't quite say out loud.

He looked around the class, and his eyes did a quick scan—maybe someone here?

Varsha: smart, opinionated, always in the mood to argue. Fatima: sweet, but very into BTS and prayer circles. Teressa: terrifying in group discussions and once broke a chair by accident.

Adam shook his head. "Nope," he muttered under his breath.

Then he remembered.

Stephany.

She was in BA English. Spoke very little Malayalam but a lot of opinions. Had that straight-cut fringe and wore Doc Martens in the Kochi sun like it was London outside. There was something different about her. Confident, funny, kind of cool.

And, importantly, she wasn't not cute.

He leaned sideways and whispered, "Pssst... Vaishnavi."

She didn't turn.

"Pssstttt."

Still nothing.

He reached out and poked her with his pen.

Vaishnavi turned slowly, giving him a look that could kill. "What?" she mouthed.

"I need a break," he whispered. "A loo break."

Vaishnavi raised one eyebrow. "During Data Structures?"

Adam winked. "You're coming too."

And like that, the plan was born. One by one, they pulled off the classic group excuse to step out. Freddy raised his eyebrows at them as they left, and Mabin barely noticed, focused on data structures.

Soon, they were walking under the banyan trees by the canteen, sipping lemon sodas. Adam cleared his throat.

"So... I was thinking..."

"Dangerous," Vaishnavi interrupted, sipping hers dramatically, the straw making that end-of-the-glass slurrrp sound.

Adam chuckled and kicked a stone off the path as they walked along the edge of the campus.

Vaishnavi glanced at him. "What now? You finally decided to grow your hair out like Abhishek Sir?"

"Maybe," he said with a smirk, then nudged her arm gently. "No, but actually... can you... maybe... help me get introduced to Stephany?"

She blinked.

Then squinted at him like he'd just said he wanted to join the seminary.

"Stephany?"

"Yeah," Adam said casually, hands in his pockets, trying not to sound too eager. "You know... your friend from BA English. She seems nice."

Vaishnavi tilted her head, quiet for a moment. A bird cooed from somewhere behind the canteen. Students passed them, laughing, shouting about a missed lab submission. But she stayed still.

There was a pause. Then her voice came out slower, softer. "You... like her?"

Adam shrugged, not meeting her eyes. "I don't know. Maybe? Just... feels like it's time, you know. Everyone has someone. Freddy does. Even Mabin's texting some girl from Visual Com."

She studied him now—not like a friend, but like someone watching puzzle pieces fall slowly into place. Her gaze wasn't jealous, not quite. It was more... thoughtful. Almost cautious.

He'd never said anything like this before. Never even hinted.

And now, here he was, asking for help to talk to a girl.

A part of her smiled.

Another part wasn't sure why her chest felt like it was sinking ever so slightly.

Adam kept talking to fill the silence. "I just think I need... someone. Like, someone I can talk to. Chill with. You know?"

Vaishnavi nodded slowly, still processing. Then suddenly—snap. Her signature grin returned, bright as ever. "Stephany's cool. You'll like her. Bit of a book snob, but at least her taste in people is decent."

Adam laughed, relieved. "Thanks, Vaish. You're the best."

She flashed him a thumbs-up, then walked ahead. "Obviously."

But as she moved forward, she bit her bottom lip, thinking.

Stephany? Really?

Adam smiled again. He wasn't sure if it was excitement... or hesitation.

But whatever it was, he told himself this:

You need this. You need to find someone. Anyone.

He needed to stop overthinking.

He needed to be normal.

By the time the next day's lunch break rolled around, Adam had started regretting asking Vaishnavi for help. Not because she wouldn't do it—oh, she would. With dramatic flair and three backup plans. But because now, every time he passed Stephany in the corridor or saw her laughing with her BA gang under the banyan tree, he felt like a lab rat walking into an arranged marriage.

Vaishnavi, on the other hand, was thriving.

"I told her you like Dostoevsky," she said, stuffing a samosa into her mouth as they sat under the rusted steel roof outside the canteen.

Adam raised an eyebrow. "I haven't even read Dostoevsky."

"She doesn't know that. Just nod if she brings it up."

"Brilliant," he muttered. "We're starting this relationship on lies and samosas."

Vaishnavi grinned. "All great love stories start with food and fake identities. You seen You've Got Mail?"

"Do I look like someone who watches romcoms?"

"Actually, yes."

Before he could argue, she waved across the walkway. "Steph! Hey!"

Adam almost choked on his water. "Wait, now?!"

Stephany, wearing a red kurti and thick-rimmed glasses, turned toward them. Her smile was polite, guarded. She walked over with the casual ease of someone who didn't get flustered easily.

"Hey," she said, brushing her hair behind her ear. "What's up?"

Vaishnavi beamed like a villain in a teen sitcom. "This is Adam. He's in CompSci. Big fan of Russian literature, loves long walks on the beach and has opinions about existential dread."

Adam wanted to melt into the pavement. He gave an awkward smile. "Hi. I don't—uh—existential dread is just part of the syllabus."

Stephany chuckled. "That's the most college thing I've heard today."

Vaishnavi nudged him under the table with her foot, as if to say See? It's working.

They talked a little. Mostly about random things—college fest coming up, the bad coffee in the canteen, how Freddy once accidentally submitted his own love letter as a C++ assignment. Stephany was easy to talk to, smart and chill. But something about it didn't click.

As she walked back to her class, Adam watched her go, feeling... blank.

"She's nice," he said.

Vaishnavi leaned back on her hands. "You sound like you're describing a salad."

"I don't know." He scratched the back of his neck. "She's cool. But..."

"But what?"

"I just thought I'd feel different."

Vaishnavi didn't say anything.

Just offered him another samosa, warm and greasy in its newspaper wrap.

Later that day, Adam was walking through the corridor near the library with Vaishnavi, the usual post-lunch stroll that neither of them admitted was just an excuse to skip Data Structures.

"So, on a scale of one to awkward," she said, twirling her pen like a wand, "how badly did you want to disappear during that Dostoevsky comment?"

Adam rolled his eyes. "I don't even know how to spell it."

"Me neither," she snorted. "We're both frauds."

He was just about to retort when it happened.

A gust of wind carried the scent before the person even appeared—earthy, musky, and unmistakably human. Warm skin in the sun. Slight cologne, probably Axe, but used sparingly. Sweat.

And just like that, Rahil walked past them.

Adam's words dissolved mid-sentence.

Rahil didn't look. Just strolled by. He was wearing a black tee that clung to his frame, hair a little messy, skin glowing with the golden confidence that came from being effortlessly liked.

Adam felt... off. His throat went dry. His limbs stiffened.

"Adam?" Vaishnavi tilted her head.

He blinked at her.

She looked concerned now. "You okay? You went white."

"I... I'm not feeling well," he muttered. "I think I need to head back. Sorry."

"Wait—did I say something wrong?"

"No, no. Not you." He tried to smile. It felt fake. "I'll text you."

Before she could respond, he turned and walked fast—maybe too fast—away from her, from the corridor, from whatever the hell just happened inside his chest.

That night, sleep refused to come.

Adam lay on his side, staring at the dark ceiling, the quiet hum of the fan overhead doing little to still the noise inside his head.

He thought about Stephany.

She was nice. Kind. Funny. Smart.

So why didn't it feel right?

He sat up, rubbing his face. The house was silent.The occasional bark of a stray dog outside, the rhythmic clunk of the old fan.

And in the silence... a thought emerged.

When was the last time I felt something real for a girl?

He traced the memories. School crushes. Random passing interests. Nothing deep. Nothing that made his stomach flip or his skin burn with awareness.

But today—when Rahil walked past, smelling like sunshine and confidence—

His hand clenched the bedsheet.

His heart was still beating weird.

Adam let out a shaky breath and sank back into the pillow.

He didn't want to name the feeling. Not yet.

He just... wasn't ready.

Not for answers.

Not for labels.

Not tonight.

CHAPTER SIX

QUESTIONS, AND SEA BREEZE

That weekend turned out to be quieter than usual, but not in the peaceful way Adam usually liked.

He sat on the veranda, doing his half-hearted version of morning exercises—stretches, a few push-ups, a little jog in place. His T-shirt stuck to his back, his forehead already glistening. But his mind wasn't in his body. It was wandering, drifting far past the coconut trees and tiled rooftops, out into a sea of strange, unanswered feelings.

He wasn't even counting reps anymore.

"Chettai!" Aleena popped her head out from the front door, ponytail swinging. "Can you do me a favour?"

Adam collapsed into a sitting position on the veranda tiles, already breathless. "Nope. Dying."

"It's literally just a—"

"Nope. Dying," he repeated, flopping backward with theatrical misery.

From the kitchen, came his mother's voice, soft but final: "Adam, just help her, da. You sit there sweating like a salted fish anyway."

Adam groaned into the floor tiles. "Fine."

Ten minutes later, he was holding Aleena's broken bicycle chain with oily fingers, muttering something about child labor laws.

The next morning, he skipped church again. This was no longer an act of rebellion—it had become ritual. A sacred one.

Mathew watched from the hallway, arms folded across his chest, as Adam left with messy hair, sleepy eyes, and yesterday's track pants. "Where are you going this early in your nightwear?" he called out.

"Pilgrimage," Adam mumbled, hopping onto his cycle and pedaling away before the questions could multiply.

The beach, once again, welcomed him with open arms. It was his temple, his therapist, his only constant.

He reached his usual spot—the familiar concrete block worn smooth by years of his presence. The waves were gentle today, curling over the shore like sighs. The smell of ocean, and early morning sun filled the air.

And then—there he was.

Ishaan.

Barefoot, standing near the waterline. Sleeveless tee, sand on his calves, sea breeze in his curls. Sunlight lit up his brown skin like bronze, his profile soft against the morning haze.

He turned, spotted Adam, and smiled like they'd planned this meeting all along.

"Hey!" he waved, jogging over with his usual boyish energy.

Adam's breath caught—not in the poetic way, just literally. He sat up straighter.

"Didn't expect to see you again so soon," Ishaan said, squinting in the sunlight.

"Yeah, I practically live here," Adam replied, suddenly hyper-aware of how unwashed his hair probably was.

They chatted—easily, gently. It was the kind of conversation that made time lose its edges. Adam learned that Ishaan had moved there just a few months ago. His father worked in the Public Works Department, and they'd been transferred from Thrissur. Ishaan was 19, a year younger, but his build made him seem older.

"I'm preparing for NEET," Ishaan said. "So, I mostly live inside textbooks now."

"Respect," Adam laughed. "I open one programming book and instantly want to throw myself into the ocean."

They both laughed.

Then, Ishaan stood and offered his hand. "Come. Let's get our feet wet. You can't sit here and act like a beach statue forever."

Adam hesitated, not because he didn't want to—but because he did.

He let Ishaan pull him up. Their fingers touched for a second longer than necessary. Maybe Adam imagined it.

The cold water hit their feet as they walked along the shoreline, ankle-deep, letting the waves lap over their toes. They talked more. Family, school memories, TV shows they hated. Adam found himself relaxing in Ishaan's presence in a way that didn't happen often—not even with Vaishnavi or Mabin.

And then Ishaan turned to him, eyes thoughtful, voice softer.

"You always this quiet? Or just with me?"

Adam blinked. "I—uh—depends?"

Ishaan smiled again. Not teasing, not smug. Just kind. "You're fun to talk to, man. I'm glad I bumped into you."

They kept walking. The breeze picked up.

Adam looked at him again, at his carefree grin and confident walk, at the way his hand flicked sand off his knee like it was nothing.

There was something about this boy.

Something that made the air feel heavier and lighter at once.

Back at his block, Adam sat again, feet drying in the sun, heart still unsure.

Ishaan had waved goodbye, saying he had to head back home before his mother started her "You'll catch a cold and fail your exam" speech.

But just before leaving, he'd turned around.

"Same time next week?" he asked, flashing that half-smile.

Adam could only nod.

As Ishaan disappeared into the morning, Adam stayed still.

That smile lingered in his head longer than it should have.

And as he pedaled back home, one thought looped through his mind:

"What's your story, Ishaan?"

CHAPTER SEVEN

ISHAAN, INTERRUPTED

Sunlight streamed in through half-closed blinds, striping the room in golden slits of warmth. A table fan whirred drowsily in the corner, scattering pages of NEET guides that lay sprawled like fallen warriors on Ishaan's cluttered study desk. Beneath a highlighter-streaked biology textbook sat a small, dented steel bowl—empty except for a few stubborn crumbs of chakka varuthathu clinging to the edges. He licked the salt from his thumb, eyes flicking over the same paragraph he'd already read three times.

"Calcium ions... neurotransmitters... synaptic cleft..." he mumbled, before slamming the book shut with a thud that didn't even startle the sleeping house.

Ishaan stretched his long arms overhead, back cracking satisfyingly. He ran a hand through his damp curls, still smelling faintly of coconut oil from the morning bath. His room was a medley of chaos and order—the football posters peeling at the corners, exam notes taped to the walls, a pair of dumbbells shoved under his cot, and a ceiling that wore glow-in-the-dark stars as if time had paused when he turned thirteen.

He stood barefoot on the cool floor, rolling his shoulders. The room, like Ishaan, was earnest. A space built from ambition and little boy dreams.

Downstairs, the air smelled faintly of toasted bread and banana fritters. His mother, Divya, was between jobs. His father, Rajesh Kumar, a stern but good-humoured PWD officer, was probably sprawled across the living room couch, snoring through the Sunday paper.

Being the only child had its perks—mostly edible ones. Ishaan grinned as he shoved a few banana fritters into his mouth, wiped his hands on the side of his shorts, and darted out the door with the familiar bounce in his steps.

The beach had become his secret escape. His new town was still unfamiliar. The streets, the shops, the uncles who stared too long, the girls who giggled too much—it was all a little loud. But the beach? The beach listened.

The usual boys were there—laughing, yelling, passing the football with the kind of energy that never needed charging. He jumped in without a word. The ball at his feet, the sun on his neck, the grit of sand between his toes—it was home, even if temporary.

It was mid-game, sweaty and breathless, when he noticed the boy.

Sitting alone, like a lost thought.

Skin pale and eyes faraway, like he was watching a different world through the waves. There was something so hauntingly quiet about him, it broke Ishaan's stride mid-pass.

He blinked, as if trying to place a face to a dream.

A football flew in the wrong direction, thudding against the boy's side.

"Oh shit."

Ishaan ran over, wiping his forehead, his bare chest sticky with sweat. "Sorry! Really sorry! .. Didn't mean to hit you!"

The boy looked up—startled, but not annoyed. His eyes met Ishaan's and for the briefest second, time became syrup. Thick and still.

They were interrupted by another boy from across the beach "He gets hit all the time! Don't worry! He's built for impact!"

Ishaan frowned and waved him off. "Go play, macha. I'll be there."

The boy rolled his eyes. "Charming."

Ishaan turned back to the boy, who was now smiling faintly, almost amused.

"It's okay. No damage done." the boy said, brushing off his shirt. His voice was softer than Ishaan expected.

Ishaan's sweat-slicked body cooled suddenly in the sea breeze. It wasn't the breeze though—it was that feeling again. The one that tugged at his chest in quiet, inconvenient ways.

He tried not to stare. "I'll get the ball and head back," motioning toward where the ball had rolled. Then, an afterthought, he turned back with a grin and said, "I'm Ishaan. New around here."

The boy nodded. "I'm Adam."

"Nice to meet you, Adam. Sorry again... Hope I didn't ruin your quiet." Ishaan smiled, trying not to look as awkward as he suddenly felt.

"Not really. Just gave me a reason to stretch," Adam replied.

Ishaan nodded, retrieved the ball, stepping backward slowly.

Adam nodded again. Just once. But it was enough.

Back at the football game, Ishaan ran harder. He kicked stronger. He laughed louder. But every few minutes, he found his eyes drifting back to that stretch of sand where Adam had sat.

Still.

Quiet.

Stunning.

He didn't know what it meant yet, but Ishaan had a strange flutter in his chest, and for once—it wasn't about the exam.

It wasn't about the future.

It was about someone... beautifully present.

CHAPTER EIGHT

BIOLOGY, BEACH, AND BLUSHES

The night was old and still, like a secret the world had already forgotten.

Ishaan sat on his bed, legs half-crossed, the last page of his chemistry notes slipping out of his fingers. The hum of the ceiling fan above cast long, lazy shadows across his room. The books were closed, lights dimmed, but his mind wouldn't rest.

Not tonight.

He lay back, arms behind his head, staring up at the faint glow-in-the-dark stars on his ceiling. He exhaled. The room smelled of ink, sweat, and jackfruit chips. But under all that, his thoughts wandered back to the sea.

Back to that boy.

Adam.

That name felt like a whisper in his chest. A name he wasn't supposed to repeat, not like this.

"I shouldn't be thinking like this," Ishaan muttered into the silence. He closed his eyes hard. "Not again."

But Adam had crept into his head like sea wind—unexpected, salty, and lingering. The boy barely spoke. Barely smiled. But there was something about him... that silence. That softness. The way he looked like he was holding a thousand words behind his lips. Ishaan had noticed the way his hair brushed his forehead. The way his voice stumbled and hushed. The way his shirt hung loose on his chest, hinting at something fragile beneath.

Ishaan pulled his blanket over his face. No. No. Stop it.

"What's wrong with me?" he whispered. "Why only boys? Why always boys?"

He turned to the wall, pressing his forehead to the coolness of it. "Why not girls like everyone else?" he asked the ceiling. Or God. Or whoever was listening.

By morning, nothing had changed. The sun rose. The same NEET class, where futures were supposed to be forged.

Except Ishaan's wasn't on a medical seat today.

It was sitting on a concrete bench by the beach.

Drinking juice with Adam. Laughing about the dumb pigeons that stole snacks. Splashing water like they were ten. Talking about life and sea and maybe... kissing.

His chest thudded.

He shook his head. Stupid. Dumb. Focus, Ishaan.

Mr. Narayanan's lecture on reproductive systems was not helping. Ishaan's mind short-circuited the moment the teacher said "testosterone." He looked at the textbook. Then the ceiling fan. Then his own thighs.

His ears turned red.

What would Adam look like under that loose tee and those lazy shorts? Would he be soft? Lean? Would he laugh if Ishaan tickled his waist? Okay. Stop. NOW.

"Bad boy," he muttered under his breath and bit his pencil.

During break, his friends were huddled around, gossiping about who was dating whom, which junior had a crush on Arun, and whether Ananya from batch C had lip fillers. Ishaan sat with them, nodding absently, eyes lost in the corridor.

A group of girls passed by, laughing too loudly, skirts swaying like blossoms. He stared at them, like he was supposed to. Tall ones, short ones, pretty ones, messy ones. All kinds.

They were beautiful. Objectively. But they didn't stir anything in him. Not like Adam did. Not like that one fleeting moment on the beach when Adam's eyes met his and it felt like a string had been tied between them.

"I could be normal," Ishaan thought. "I could choose one of these girls. Date. Lie. Pretend."

But his throat tightened at the thought. He felt cold.

What if Adam never looked at him that way? What if he was imagining it all? What if this was just a painful, lonely fantasy? What if this thing inside him—this wild, aching love—was meant to stay hidden forever?

He hated that part the most. The hiding. The quiet pretending.

Why did God make him this way when He made so many girls for boys to love?

Why Adam? Why this boy who barely knew him, barely spoke?

But Ishaan felt it. Somewhere deep and sure. This wasn't just a crush. It was something older. Something raw.

Something he had no words for yet.

He didn't need a reason. He just wanted to know him.
And maybe—just maybe—be known back

CHAPTER NINE

TREMORS IN THE LOCKER ROOM

That week was not kind to Adam.

Everything felt like it was running too fast or standing too still. His thoughts never settled. He avoided Stephany in the corridors—even when she smiled. And when they accidentally ran into each other near the canteen, it was all just... awkward filler words.

"Oh hey!"

"Hey!"

"You... had lunch?"

"Yeah... you?"

And silence would drop like fog.

His friends noticed too. Freddy had stopped cracking jokes around him. Mabin tried talking but Adam kept it short. But it was Vaishnavi who faced the worst of it. Every time she asked him anything, Adam snapped. A grunt. A rolled eye. He didn't mean it. But he didn't stop either.

Until something shifted.

The list was pinned on the board that morning. The college cricket team. Adam's name was there, bold and neat. Adam Mathew. Opening Batsman.

He stared at it for a whole minute. His heart beating like it was mid-run.

By lunch, Vaishnavi had already heard. She passed by him at first, giving him a mock-cold shoulder. But when he followed her and tapped her hand, she turned and grabbed him in a fierce hug.

"You idiot," she whispered, "congratulations."

That was the first smile Adam truly meant in days.

The next few days were a blur of practices, field drills, bat swings, and light banter. He slowly reconnected with his group—joking with Mabin, pulling Freddy's leg, and even texting Stephany.

Stephany was nice. Calm. She laughed at his awkward puns and listened when he rambled about batting techniques and video editing. They shared a decent rhythm.

But that was it. Decent. Friendly. Familiar.

It was never electric.

Never dizzying.

The day of his first full team practice arrived.

Adam wore his college jersey like it was armour—his name stitched behind his shoulder blades. He joined the group under the scorching sun. The field was loud with energy, sneakers scraping against turf, balls thudding into gloves, coaches barking out plays.

And then came Rahil.

The captain. Towering, confident, sweaty already from a warm-up run. His body strong like it had no memory of weakness.

"Adam," the coach called, waving him forward. "You're opening today. Let's see what you've got."

Rahil jogged over, patted Adam's shoulder with his wide, firm hands. "Welcome to the team, champ. Don't disappoint."

The warmth from that touch rushed straight into Adam's skin. A tremble. Almost invisible. But it was there.

"Thanks," Adam managed, not meeting his eyes.

Bat in hand, he walked to the crease, trying to focus. To breathe. And when the ball came, he struck. Straight, neat, cracking against the turf. Applause echoed. Mabin screamed in pride from the benches.

For a moment, Adam felt like himself again. Capable. Sure. Steady.

But it didn't last.

Later, in the locker room, the air was thick with sweat, deodorant, and end-of-practice fatigue. Adam walked into the washroom, wiping his face with a towel.

And there he was.

Rahil.

Half-naked, muscles glistening, towel low on his waist. His back was broad, his chest rising and falling in a slow, heavy rhythm.

Adam's breath hitched. His hands turned cold.

Rahil noticed him. Walked over slowly. Casual. Confident.

"Good shots today," he said, running a hand through his damp hair. "You've got style."

Adam mumbled something like a "thanks," eyes focused anywhere but on Rahil's body.

Then Rahil leaned in, just enough to send a ripple down Adam's spine. His voice was low, warm against Adam's ear.

"There's a party at my place. You and your buddy Mabin should come."

Adam nodded, his face burning.

But Rahil wasn't done.

He stepped back slightly, just enough to meet Adam's eyes. Then he smiled—half a smirk, half a secret.

"I know the way you look at me."

He winked. And walked away.

Adam didn't move. Didn't blink.

The world stood still as the tiled floor spun beneath him. Sighed!

Adam came back to his senses. Or did he?

He felt euphoric and quickly packed his gym bag, ready to run off to his home before more embarassment.

CHAPTER TEN

FRIDAY NIGHTS AND FIRST TASTES

It was a Friday evening stitched with adrenaline.

Adam stood in front of his mirror for the fifth time, adjusting the collar of his best casual shirt. A deep navy, ironed with care. He ran his hands through his straight hair, added a little texture, and sprayed two pumps of his favorite cologne—just enough to feel confident but not like he was trying too hard.

In the corner of the room, his backpack was stuffed with an extra T-shirt and some old textbooks—a prop for the sleepover lie.

"Going to Mabin's to study," he had said.
His mom believed him. His dad barely nodded.

And yet, as he slipped out into the humid night, guilt pressed lightly on his chest.

But excitement outshouted everything else.

He met Mabin near the old bakery junction. Mabin was already grinning, balancing a packet of chips on his cycle's handlebar.

"You look like a walking deodorant ad," Mabin teased. Adam smirked. "Shut up and pedal."

They rode together, weaving through the narrow streets. The town buzzed with the usual weekend rhythm—shop lights flickering, fishermen returning home, teenagers on bikes laughing too loudly.

And then came the bungalow.

Rahil's house.

It's been only seven. Music thumped through the walls. The gate was half open, like it had been asked to stay that way.

Inside, it was chaos and colour.

Boys and girls lounged on bean bags and danced in corners. Bottles clinked. Laughter echoed. Someone played an old Malayalam remix, and someone else tried to beatbox.

Adam took it all in, wide-eyed.

Then—

"Adam?"

He turned. Stephany. In a red crop top, a coke in hand, her smile warm but... complicated.

"Oh, hey!"

"I didn't know you were coming."

Before Adam could respond, a boy—tall, dusky, with a tattoo on his collarbone—came up and slipped his arm around Stephany's waist.

"Hey babe," he said, without acknowledging Adam.

Adam smiled, weakly. "So... your boyfriend."

Stephany nodded, catching his tone. "Yeah. His name's Nihal."

And that was that.

It hurt—more from the theatre he had built in his head than from actual heartbreak.

But strangely, it also lifted something off his shoulders.

He no longer had to pretend.

Later, Rahil found him.

With a beer bottle in one hand and his signature charm in the other, Rahil raised a mock toast. "To the new boy in our cricket team—Adam!"

The group cheered. Someone handed him a can. He took a polite sip, then another. The warmth hit him slowly—like a secret being told in waves.

Food followed. Games. Silly dares. Songs half-remembered. People leaning on couches, limbs tangling with laughter. Few girls, including Stephany had already left.

Adam was dizzy—but not from the alcohol, or parting Stephany.

He needed air.

Outside, the night had cooled. The sky wore stars like a shawl, and the trees whispered in sea breeze.

Adam leaned on the railing of the balcony. Silence wrapped around him.

Then, footsteps.

Rahil.

He joined Adam with a casual ease. "Needed a break too?"

Adam nodded. "It's loud in there."

They stood together, shoulder to shoulder, looking into the night.

"You okay?" Rahil asked.

"I think so. Just... this is all new."

Rahil lit a cigarette, took a drag, and exhaled slowly. "You're different, Adam."

Adam chuckled. "Everyone says that when they don't know what to say next."

Rahil looked at him, quiet for a moment.

Then, without a word, he leaned in.

And kissed him.

Soft. Slow. Sure

Adam froze. His lips parted in shock.

But then...

He felt it.

Warmth. Fire. A sweetness that wasn't in the drink.

He kissed back—hesitant at first, then leaning in, lost in the moment. Their lips moved slowly, curiously, like two boys learning a language that felt familiar but forbidden.

Rahil's hand gently found Adam's waist, pulling him closer. Their breaths became uneven. Adam's fingers, slightly trembling, found the hem of Rahil's shirt.

"Come," Rahil whispered, voice husky. He led Adam quietly through the house, past the sleepy hum of the party, into his room.

The door clicked shut behind them.

The room was dimly lit—soft shadows, clothes strewn, the scent of cologne and sweat lingering in the air.

They stood there for a second, just breathing.

Then, slowly, Rahil reached out. His hands moved to the buttons of Adam's shirt. One by one, they came undone, his eyes never leaving Adam's..

There was a moment—a pause—where both of them looked at each other, unsure, unspoken questions floating in the silence.

But when their bodies met again, it was full of hunger and release.

They found each other in hurried touches and nervous laughter, in skin against skin and long, deep breaths. It wasn't perfect, but it was real. Messy. Tender.

That night, something in Adam shifted.

He didn't know what this meant, or what would follow.

But for the first time, he didn't feel like running away from himself.

He felt... seen.

Held.

Alive.

CHAPTER ELEVEN

THE SHAME

Adam stirred awake to the faint throb in his head and the weight of something he couldn't place—not entirely hangover, not entirely peace. His bedsheet was tangled around his legs, his shirt twisted, his body sore in unfamiliar places.

The clock read 4:06 PM.

He blinked.

He remembered reaching home around 8 that morning, eyes half-shut, ignoring his mother's call from the kitchen. He had gone straight to his room and crashed onto the bed.

Now, as he rolled over, a scent drifted up from his skin and his pillow—faint, musky, familiar.

Rahil.

Adam smiled... and then, it hit him.

What did I do?

Images from the night came rushing in. The way Rahil touched him, the way he kissed back, the heat, the laughter, the quiet, the tremble. He remembered bending forward, offering himself like he'd never done before.

He wanted it. Every part of it.

But now...

Now he wasn't sure how to carry it.

He sat on the edge of his bed, buried his face in his palms, and sat there for a long time. Then, silently, he pulled himself to the bathroom and turned on the shower.

The water didn't wash the thoughts away.

He scrubbed harder anyway.

Later, freshly dressed, hair still damp, he stomped downstairs and poured himself a glass of tea.

His father was sitting on the armchair, reading the newspaper. He barely looked up.

"Someone had a fun night," Mathew said, his voice dipped in sarcasm.

Adam took a long sip of tea. "Played video games all night. Felt dizzy this morning."

His father hummed nonchalantly and turned a page. Adam grabbed his cycle keys and walked out before any more questions followed.

The beach welcomed him like an old friend. The sea, generous and infinite, never asked questions.

He sat on his usual concrete seat, watching the waves lazily fold over each other, a golden haze cast over the water by the descending sun.

He replayed everything.

The kiss. The touch. The pleasure.

The shame.

He wanted it, yes. But he also wanted to not feel this ache in his chest. This guilt. This fear that he was now... different. That things wouldn't go back to how they were.

He exhaled.

That's when he saw him.

Ishaan—shirtless, sweaty, sprinting across the sand, football in hand, sun dripping off his skin.

"Hi Adam!" Ishaan beamed, jogging toward him. His smile was wild and honest.

Adam blinked. He managed a half-smile.

"Hey," he said quietly.

"You okay?" Ishaan asked, dropping beside him. "You look like you watched a horror movie in Malayalam."

Adam let out a small laugh.

Ishaan poked him playfully, then launched into stories about the beach football match, about how one guy tripped over a crab, and how another ran straight into the water chasing the ball.

Bit by bit, Adam's walls began to crumble. He laughed. He teased back. He let go—just enough.

As the sun dipped closer to the water, painting the sea orange and violet, they both fell into a warm silence.

Adam glanced at Ishaan.

"It's nice... talking with you," he said.

Ishaan looked at him, his cheeks faintly red. "I feel the same. Honestly, I think I found a real friend in this strange new town."

There was a pause. Then Ishaan added, "Come to my house sometime? Amma makes crazy good pazham pori."

Adam hesitated. His heart still fluttered with ghosts.

But he nodded. "Yeah... I'd like that."

In that moment, for the first time since last night, Rahil faded from his mind.

Only the waves, the sunset, and Ishaan remained.

CHAPTER TWELVE

PAZHAM PORI & WARMTH

After the sun dipped beyond the sea and the orange melted into blue, Ishaan picked up his football and grinned at Adam.

"Come over," he said. "My mom's been on a pazham pori streak. And you've earned one."

Adam hesitated for a second, then nodded. Something about Ishaan made it easy to say yes.

Ishaan's home sat tucked behind a row of jasmine hedges. It was a modest two-story house with fading blue paint, the kind that smelled of turmeric, old photo albums, and years of evening prayers.

"Amma! Appa!" Ishaan called out as they stepped in. "This is Adam, my beachmate."

Rajesh, his father, stepped out from the hall wearing a white lungi and a grin. "So you're the guy who's been making Ishaan smile like an idiot all week?"

"Appa!" Ishaan groaned, shoving him playfully.

Divya emerged from the kitchen in a loose cotton nightie, wiping her hands on her towel.

"Welcome, mone," she smiled. "Come, sit. Tea?"

Before Adam could say yes or no, she'd already vanished back to the kitchen. Ishaan rolled his eyes and gestured toward the dining table.

Two steaming cups of tea. A plate full of golden, crispy pazham pori.

Adam bit into one and let out a low, surprised mmm.

Ishaan laughed. "Told you."

They munched and chatted under the ceiling fan, talking about school, NEET prep, and how Ishaan once accidentally submitted a blank answer sheet in 8th grade. Rajesh chipped in with jokes. Divya quietly observed Adam—her eyes gentle, curious.

Later, Ishaan dragged Adam upstairs to his room.

It was exactly what Adam expected.

Textbooks piled on the desk, random sticky notes on the walls, a broken plastic football trophy gathering dust on the corner shelf. The air smelled like fresh detergent, coconut oil, and boy.

Adam sat cautiously on the edge of the bed, only to spot a crumpled black underwear lying in the center.

"Shit—sorry!" Ishaan gasped, quickly scooping it up and flinging it under the bed like it never existed.

Adam burst into laughter.

"Stop laughing!" Ishaan groaned, his ears pink.

"I'm honoured," Adam said between chuckles. "A true glimpse into your royal chambers."

They sat and talked more—about the beach, their favourite Malayalam movies, dumb things their parents say.

Then Ishaan picked up his phone. "Smile."

Click.

Adam was caught mid-laugh, head tilted, eyes half-shut.

Another one—both of them, cheeks pressed, Ishaan holding a half-eaten pazham pori in the corner of the frame.

Ishaan opened Instagram. A new Story went up:

— Beach Vibes

— Amma's pazham pori supremacy

— New buddy in town

Adam looked over at the screen and smiled.

It felt... unreal. Comfortably unreal. Like he'd known Ishaan for years instead of weeks.

There was no pressure. No tremble. No chase.

Just this... warm, dumb, beautiful peace.

CHAPTER THIRTEEN

NAMES FOR THINGS

Adam sat in the middle row of the classroom, eyes staring at the board, but his mind miles away. The fan hummed above like a distant warning. Notes were being dictated, pens were scribbling, someone was whispering answers behind him.

But Adam? He sat frozen, a quiet tremble in his fingers, still stuck somewhere between Rahil's bed and the cold floor of his room.

Did it really happen?

Yes.

He could still feel it.

The scent of Rahil.

The way his heart had raced, then crashed.

It wasn't just the kiss.

It was the silence after.

The shrug from Rahil in the corridor.

The way he avoided Adam's eyes the entire week.

Like nothing happened.

Like Adam was a smudge on his memory.

The bell rang, loud and final.

Adam jumped, startled. His eyes searched for Rahil as students began to leave. There he was, laughing with his senior friends, his voice louder than necessary.

Adam rushed to him, anxiety like a wave rising in his throat.

"Hey... Rahil. Can we talk?"

Rahil turned, paused for a second. Then the smile faded. "What for?"

Adam swallowed. "About that night..."

"That night?" Rahil raised an eyebrow, cocking his head. "What night?"

"Please," Adam whispered. "I just—need to understand."

Rahil leaned in closer, eyes sharp. "Nothing happened, okay? And if you open your mouth about this to anyone, I'll break your fucking bones. Got it?"

Adam blinked, stunned. Something inside him shattered.

"Whore," Rahil muttered under his breath as he walked away.

Adam stood still in the hallway as the crowd moved past him. He felt like his skin didn't fit anymore. His mouth was dry. His eyes, wet. His legs were heavy.

He walked out, numb.

Vaishnavi called after him. Freddy waved from the field.

He didn't stop.

He couldn't.

That night, Adam lay in his bed, arms folded under his head, staring at the clunky fan on the ceiling.

He wanted to scream.

What am I? Why did I let that happen?

No, wait.

I wanted it. I leaned in. I kissed him back.

It wasn't an accident.

It wasn't a phase.

It wasn't the liquor.

It was him.

The way he looked at boys in the locker room.

The way he felt uneasy when his friends talked about their crushes on girls.

The way he followed shirtless models and dancers on Instagram, not just for aesthetics, but because they made his heart race.

I'm gay.

There. He whispered it to himself.

The word tasted foreign and familiar at once.

It echoed in the stillness of his room.

He curled up and cried—not because he was ashamed anymore, but because it finally made sense.

The next day, he saw Rahil again.

Same college corridor.

Same sharp light falling through the windows.

But this time, Adam wasn't trembling.

He had rehearsed it all night in his head—

the words,

the tone,

the pace of his breath.

Rahil was leaning against the notice board, casually scrolling through his phone, pretending not to notice Adam approaching.

"Hey," Adam said, his voice calm but firm.

Rahil glanced up, eyebrows tightening for a moment. There was a flicker of something—fear, maybe, or guilt—but it vanished as quickly as it came.

"I'm not going to tell anyone. Don't worry," Adam said.

Rahil's jaw clenched.

A brief silence passed between them, loud in its own way.

Adam continued, "But what you did... and how you treated me..."

His throat tightened.

He swallowed, hard.

"...was cruel."

Rahil's lips parted like he wanted to speak—an excuse, a deflection, maybe even an apology—but Adam had already turned.

He walked away before Rahil could say anything.

Because this time, Adam wasn't waiting for closure.

He was writing his own.

But the weight didn't lift. Not right away.

That day at lunch, Adam sat with his friends, quiet and withdrawn. Vaishnavi nudged him playfully, Freddy cracked a joke, but Adam just stared at his food.

Then, without warning, he burst into tears.

"Hey—hey, Adam, what happened?" Vaishnavi panicked, grabbing his hand.

Freddy looked confused, alarmed.

"I don't know," Adam lied.

Because how do you explain a heartbreak you're not allowed to grieve?

CHAPTER FOURTEEN

UNSPOKEN THINGS

Saturday afternoons were sacred for group study.

It was the one time of the week where books were opened, snacks were shared, and very little studying actually happened.

Adam had been hesitant to go. But Mabin had texted "Don't be a ghost again" and Freddy had followed up with a "Vaishnavi's mom is making biryani."

So... he showed up.

Vaishnavi's house had that lived-in warmth: mismatched cushions, soft lighting, the smell of turmeric and incense wafting in from the kitchen. Freddy was already there, fiddling with the Wi-Fi, and Mabin was snacking on something crunchy.

Adam nodded hello to everyone and slumped into the bean bag, trying to look less... haunted.

After some light mockery, some math, and a lot of zero progress, Freddy got a call from his mom and Mabin decided to leave early for a cousin's birthday.

It was just Adam and Vaishnavi now.

She sat cross-legged on the floor, hair tied up in her usual lazy bun, scrolling through something while sipping chai.

"You okay now?" she asked, looking up at him with that soft, non-judgmental gaze she always saved for the people she truly cared about.

Adam didn't answer immediately. He looked at the half-empty chai cup in his hand.

"I need to tell you something," he said finally. "But you'll hate me for it."

Vaishnavi raised an eyebrow. "I once ate an entire chicken pizza alone and blamed Freddy. So, trust me, I can handle whatever you're about to say."

Adam half-laughed. Then sighed.

He hesitated.

And then he told her. Not everything in explicit detail—but enough. The party. Rahil. What happened. How he felt. The shame. The realisation. The heartbreak.

Vaishnavi sat very still. Listening. Letting him finish.

And then... she laughed.

"Wait, you thought I'd hate you for this?" she said, tossing a pillow at him. "Adam, come on. I had doubts already."

Adam blinked. "Wait... what?"

She leaned back, arms crossed smugly. "You avoided Stephany like she had the flu. And after that fallout? Your whole 'I like her' act had so many plot holes it could be a Netflix drama."

That made Adam laugh properly. The tension cracked.

"But seriously," she said, a little gentler, "thank you for telling me. That takes guts."

Adam exhaled. "I thought you'd stop talking to me."

"Why? Because you're gay? Please. If you were straight," she said dramatically, "you would've totally fallen in love with me. I mean, look at me."

Adam laughed so hard he had to clutch his stomach. But then... the realisation hit.

"Oh."

Vaishnavi smiled, but her eyes softened. "Yeah. I did have a thing for you, once."

Adam looked down. "I'm sorry. I didn't know. I never meant to—"

"I know," she cut in. "You never gave me mixed signals. I just... liked you because you were kind. And real. And always remembered my chai order."

He looked at her, eyes slightly wet now.

"Thank you," he said. "For still being here."

"Always," she replied, nudging his shoulder. "And for the record, you're not alone in this. You never were."

They sat like that, in the fading afternoon light, with an old fan creaking above them and a quiet bond between them that somehow felt stronger than ever.

CHAPTER FIFTEEN

MORNING TIDES & MESSY TRUTHS

Sunday mornings had a rhythm of their own.

The beach was quieter, the waves gentler, and the skies lazy in their stretch of pastel blue and faded orange.

Adam sat alone on his usual concrete perch, legs folded, staring at the ocean. There was a lightness inside him—a kind of soft calm—after opening up to Vaishnavi the day before. But the weight of Rahil's betrayal still anchored him. He didn't know how to forgive himself for wanting something real and ending up with something that felt... used.

He took a deep breath, salty air filling his lungs.

And then—

"Hey, beach boy," a familiar voice called.

Adam looked up. And there he was.

Ishaan.

But not the usual sweaty football version of him. Today, Ishaan wore a crisp pale-blue shirt, sleeves rolled up, beige linen trousers, and his curls had actually been tamed—well, mostly. He even wore cologne—something fruity and warm, like orange blossoms meeting vanilla.

Adam blinked. "Wow. You clean up well."

Ishaan grinned. "You say that like you're surprised."

"I am."

Ishaan laughed, then without hesitation, hugged Adam. It was brief but full of something warm. Reassurance, maybe.

They sat quietly on the warm concrete edge near the beach, the ocean in front of them shimmering like a mood board neither of them could read.

The salty wind danced in Adam's hair as he turned to Ishaan and asked softly, "What is love, Ishaan?"

Ishaan blinked, caught off-guard by the question. "Whoa," he said, smiling. "That's a lot for a Sunday morning."

Adam looked away, his voice barely audible, "I just... need to know. I've been so confused lately. About everything."

Ishaan nodded. He turned towards Adam and asked, "Can I ask you something first?"

Adam looked back at him and nodded.

"Have you ever felt safe around someone? Like... you could show them your weirdest self and they'd still stick around?"

Adam thought for a moment. His eyes flicked with memories. "Yes. A couple of times... maybe."

Ishaan continued, "And have you ever wanted to listen to someone—not to reply, not to impress—but just because their voice made your day feel a little less... lonely?"

Adam nodded again, this time slowly.

"Then maybe... you already know what love feels like."

He turned toward the sea, watching a couple walk barefoot on the wet sand, laughing at nothing.

"I think love isn't a single thing. It's a recipe, you know?" Ishaan's voice softened. "It's built on little layers."

"Like?"

"Like respect, first of all," Ishaan said. "My parents fight sometimes, and I used to think that meant something was wrong. But the thing is... even when they're mad, my dad still makes tea for my mom every morning. That's respect. You can disagree, but you never disrespect."

Adam listened, eyes fixed on Ishaan, like each word was stitching something back together inside him.

"Then there's trust," Ishaan said, turning serious. "One time in school, I broke something expensive in the lab. I was so scared I almost ran away. But my best friend saw me panicking. And instead of judging or exposing me, he just stood beside me and said, 'Let's go talk to the teacher. I'm with you.' That moment? That was trust. No conditions, no questions."

Adam lowered his eyes. That hit home.

"Communication," Ishaan added. "This one's hard. Everyone talks, right? But how many people listen?" He paused. "I've seen couples who look perfect on Instagram, but in real life, they're just... pretending. If you can't talk about your fears, your confusions, your stupid crushes... is that really love?"

Adam swallowed hard.

"And lastly," Ishaan's voice went gentle, almost a whisper, "love is valid—no matter what form it takes. Love is when your heart slows down when they smile. It doesn't need approval. It just is."

Adam's mind was racing. He took a deep breath, his heart pounding, and finally, he spoke, "You explained it so well, Ishaan. I... I think I finally get it. I know where I went wrong now."

For the first time that day, he felt something settle in his chest, like a weight lifting. He smiled at Ishaan, thankful for his words.

But just as he was about to say more, he noticed something that stopped him in his tracks. Ishaan's eyes were wet. His lips trembled.

"Ishaan?" Adam asked softly, his voice laced with concern.

Ishaan wiped his face quickly, looking away. "I'm... I'm fine," he said, his voice strained. He took a shaky breath, turning to face the sun. "I've just... been keeping a lot in."

Adam could feel the air between them shift, the mood growing heavier. But before he could say anything, Ishaan stood abruptly, wiping his face one last time with a hand. "I... I need to go," he muttered, his voice thick with something unspoken. "See you, Adam."

Adam sat there, watching Ishaan walk away, his heart caught between the weight of the conversation and the mystery of what had just unfolded. He didn't understand the tears, but he could feel them, and they made him question everything all over again.

THE BOY FROM THE BUS SHED

A few years ago, Ishaan had a crew cut that didn't really flatter him and skin fairer than now, before sun and sweat turned him golden. He waited at the dusty bus shed with his headphones on, playing the same Tamil playlist for the hundredth time. His eyes scanned the road, eager, searching—for him.

Adithya, or Adhi as Ishaan fondly called him, was his best friend since before they even knew how to spell friendship. They grew up together—tuition classes, football at the temple ground, sharing ice creams and stupid secrets. They were two peas in a pod—except for one thing.

Where Ishaan questioned everything, Adhi followed what he was told. Ishaan was liberal, curious, open to change. Adhi was from an affluent, tight-knit, conservative family and carried the weight of that tradition in the way he thought, spoke, and moved.

That day, they were going to a local dance event at the town hall. Ishaan loved watching performances—folk, bharatanatyam, street, anything really. The colors, the rhythm, the stories told through movement—it all fascinated him.

When they reached, the hall was buzzing. The lights dimmed, the show began. Ishaan kept nudging Adhi during the performances—"Did you see that footwork?", "This guy's expressions are killer!" Adhi smiled mildly, nodding along.

Afterward, they stopped at the bakery next to the bus stand. Ishaan had his usual egg puff and lime juice, cheeks glowing from the performance high.

"The boys today..." Ishaan began, sipping his drink, "they were absolutely amazing. Especially that bharatanatyam guy—he owned the stage."

Adhi chuckled. "Yeah, they were good. So good that they must be gay."

The straw in Ishaan's mouth froze. "What?"

Adhi shrugged. "I mean, not in a bad way. Just saying. Boys dancing like that? Come on. Classical dance, especially. That's kinda..."

"That's kinda what?" Ishaan's voice sharpened.

"Well, not straight."

Ishaan blinked, stunned. "Do you even hear yourself? That's such a lazy stereotype. So every guy who dances is gay? What kind of backward logic is that?"

Adhi leaned back, nonchalant. "I didn't say every dancer. Just... most classical ones. It's a thing, bro. Don't overreact."

"Wow." Ishaan's throat tightened. "You sound exactly like those uncles on WhatsApp who think jeans make girls immoral."

The tension crackled. Passersby, unaware, moved past them while their friendship stood still.

"And even if they were gay?" Ishaan's voice dropped, heavy and firm. "What's wrong with that?"

Adhi sighed. "Nothing's wrong. I mean, to each their own. But it's not natural, Ishaan. You're not supposed to be that way."

Ishaan stared at him, breath shallow. His heartbeat was deafening. His lips trembled but he held his ground.

"I am," he said softly. "I'm gay, Adhi."

Adhi's face went blank. Then he laughed, nervously. "Oh shut up. You're not serious."

"I am. I've known for a while now. And I told you because I thought... if anyone, you'd understand."

Adhi rubbed his neck. "Man, it's probably just a phase. Like... I don't know. Hormones. You'll grow out of it."

"I won't. This isn't a phase. This is who I am."

Adhi didn't say anything after that. They parted ways that night in silence.

In the days that followed, something began to change.

At school, Adhi started avoiding him. No more saved seats. No more lunch chats. No more shared jokes. He drifted into a different circle—one that made fun of the very boys they used to be.

Ishaan tried pretending it didn't bother him. But it tore him apart inside.

One day, unable to take it anymore, he confronted Adhi behind the school canteen. "Why are you doing this? I'm still the same person. I'm still me."

Adhi's face twisted. "No, you're not. You chose to be that. And now you want me to be okay with it?"

"I didn't choose anything," Ishaan yelled, "I just finally told you the truth!"

Adhi's eyes narrowed. "You disgust me."

And that was it. Their story ended in three words.

Ishaan didn't go back to class that day. He took the long route home and walked straight into his mother's arms. He wept. His mother held him close, gently rubbing his back, not knowing what had broken her boy.

He never told her. Not that day.

But that day, Ishaan learned something about love. That sometimes, it doesn't survive truth. But also—that truth is still worth telling.

The fan hummed above him, slow and steady.

Ishaan sat on the edge of his bed, elbows on knees, staring at the wall. The shadows of the window grill painted lines across his floor, sharp and soft, like the memories in his head.

"You disgust me."

Adhi's voice.

Still so loud.

Still so final.

The words were years old now, but they hadn't aged. They hadn't mellowed or faded. They just... stayed. Like scars on skin no one could see.

Ishaan rubbed his hands together, trying to shake the cold that wasn't really there.

He rolled onto his bed, curled up tight, and forced his eyes shut.

He needed sleep.

He needed peace.

He needed to forget.

But the mind had its own theatre.

And suddenly, Adhi was gone.

In his place...

was Adam.

Adam, with his soft, unruly hair that always looked like the wind loved playing with it.

Adam, with skin so pale and eyes so full of questions it made Ishaan want to sit next to him forever, just to help him find the answers.

Adam, with lips that looked like they'd never yelled in anger, only whispered truth and longing.

Adam, with the body that moved like it held secrets and stories, ones that made Ishaan feel things he'd locked away for years.

He opened his eyes.

The room was still.

The silence had weight.

And in that silence, Ishaan whispered into the dark, "I think I'm in love."

And the moment he said it, the fear came rushing in.

Because love wasn't simple.

Not for people like him.

For someone like Ishaan, love wasn't candlelight and grand gestures.

It was hidden glances.

It was quiet prayers.

It was knowing that even if your heart screams, your mouth must whisper.

He buried his face into the pillow.

This was the plight.

Of every boy who loved differently.

Who loved quietly.

Who loved in fear.

To know love.

To feel love.

And to be terrified of what that love could cost.

But in that fear... there was also something else.

Hope.

Because this time, the boy in his mind wasn't a ghost from the past.

He was real.

He was here.

And maybe—just maybe—he wouldn't run.

CHAPTER SEVENTEEN

UNDER THE EVENING SKY

The clink of cutlery echoed in the dining room.
Adam sat silently at the table, pushing rice around his plate.
Chewing slowly.
Swallowing slower.

His mother had already cleared her plate and left.
Only the ceiling fan and a lukewarm curry remained.

Across the table, Mathew watched him. Quietly.
Adam didn't notice. Or maybe he did—but didn't care.

The silence stretched until the last spoon dropped.

"Come."
Mathew's voice, low and steady.

They stepped out into the courtyard.

The sky was indigo now, the last trace of the sun bleeding behind the rooftops.
Crickets sang softly.
A light breeze rustled the jackfruit tree near the gate.

Mathew leaned against the pillar. Adam stood awkwardly, eyes on the gravel.

"You've been... off, for weeks now," Mathew said gently.
"Like you're carrying something too big for your chest."

Adam didn't reply.

Mathew looked up at the stars. "What is it, mone? Talk to me."

Adam's lips parted. Closed. Parted again.

Then—

"Apacha..."

A pause. A tremble in the voice.

"If someone did something that society thinks is wrong... but deep inside, they know it's true—something kind and human—would you still love them?"

Mathew turned to him slowly.

"Society doesn't always know what's right," he said. "But humanity does. And you... do. You follow your truth. And you will always have my love."

That was it.

That was all Adam needed.

He took a breath so deep it shook his shoulders.

And finally, he said it.

"Apacha... I'm gay."

"I like boys."

"This is me."

"I tried, I really did... to be what they call 'normal'. To blend in. To fit in. But I can't."

"I don't want to hide anymore."

"You can hate me if you want. But I'm not afraid anymore."

The words fell between them.

Heavy.

Naked.

Freeing.

Mathew didn't flinch.

He walked toward Adam and placed a hand on his shoulder.

"I knew."

Adam looked up, stunned.

"I've known, son. I'm your father. I'm supposed to know.
You don't have to say a word sometimes.
I've seen you struggle, and it broke my heart that you had
to walk through this alone."

Adam's eyes filled. He bit his lip hard.

Mathew pulled him into a hug.

"I don't care who you love. I care how you love.
And if you do it with honesty and kindness,
then I am proud of you."

Adam crumbled into his father's arms.

The stars above blinked silently.

The night didn't change.

But Adam did.

That night, for the first time in his life—
He felt free.

CHAPTER EIGHTEEN

BEFORE THE SUNSET ENDS

Adam was restless the next day..

The sun was out, the canteen buzzed with laughter, but inside him, everything felt still—
like a pause button had been pressed on the world.

He sat alone near the steps of the library when Vaishnavi spotted him.

She didn't speak right away.
Just sat next to him with her cold coffee.

After a long silence, Adam said softly,
"V... I think I'm in love."

Vaishnavi turned, raising an eyebrow with a mischievous grin.
"Oh? Anyone I know?"

Adam looked down, nervous.

"It's Ishaan."

There was a pause.

Not the kind that brings judgment.
But the kind that holds space for truth.

Vaishnavi blinked. Then her face softened.

"I knew it," she whispered. "The way you speak about him... it's different."

Adam's eyes welled up.

"I'm scared, Vaishu. What if it ruins everything? What if he doesn't feel the same? What if I'm wrong again..."

She placed her hand on his.

"Adam. You've spent enough time running away from your feelings."

"You deserve to feel this. You deserve to be happy."

"And if you love him—tell him. Don't wait for a perfect day. Just do it. Today."

She smiled.

"And if it crashes, you have me to come cry to."

Adam chuckled through his tears.

And in that moment, he knew—
he wasn't alone anymore.

That evening, he didn't wait.

The moment college got over, Adam rushed home, changed into his favorite outfit, and hopped onto his cycle. His heart was thudding with anticipation, hands gripping the handlebar tighter than usual.

He wasn't sure if it was courage or impulse—but he knew one thing: he couldn't hold it in any longer.

He cycled fast.

The wind slicing past him, his heart louder than the traffic—Adam reached the beach just before sunset.

This time, he sat on his favorite concrete not as a confused boy,
but as someone who had finally accepted his heart.

He saw him.

Ishaan.

Walking alone through the sand in his messy sleeveless shirt, his curls wild, his smile absent—until he spotted Adam.

Adam jumped up and waved.

Ishaan skipped his football group and made his way straight to him.

Before he could speak, Adam said—

"It's okay if you're not ready to talk about the other day. I won't force you."

"But I need to say something."

"Walk with me?"

They walked in silence, the waves whispering near their feet.

And then Adam stopped.

"I've been through so much lately. So many questions."

"But the one thing that's clear to me is you."

"Ishaan, I've never felt this safe, this free, with anyone else."

Adam paused and took and deep breathe.

"I'm in love with you. Ishaan". Adam continued.

"I want to know all of you—your secrets, your laughter, your quiet pain."

"I want to walk beside you, through every chapter."

"I don't care who's watching. I'm choosing you."

Ishaan stood frozen.

His eyes were shimmering.

He stepped forward, hands trembling, and held Adam's face gently.

"Oh! Dear Adam!"

And then, without hesitation—

Ishaan kissed Adam.

Under the golden sky, in front of the world,
he kissed the boy he thought he'd never be brave enough to love.

Gasps echoed.

A football rolled by and stopped.
Tourists blinked. Vendors went quiet.
But for Adam and Ishaan—time didn't exist.
Only them.
As they slowly pulled apart, Ishaan whispered:
"I love you, daa. I think I always have."
Adam's heart broke open.
The waves roared with joy.
The wind carried whispers of their names.
They embraced like a silhouette against the sunset—two boys, finally free in their own skin.
Not bothered by the world around them
Because finally, they knew...
They were not wrong. They were not alone.
They were in love. And that was enough.

Epilogue

It's been a year since that sunset.

Adam still visits the beach on Sundays.

Sometimes with Ishaan. Sometimes alone.

Sometimes just to sit on his favourite concrete and watch the waves, remembering the boy he used to be—scared, silent, searching.

Now, he smiles more.

He still overthinks, still bites his nails during exams, still argues with Vaishnavi about silly things—but he no longer carries the weight of shame.

Ishaan is still messy, still chaotic, still smells like old books and wild cologne.

He hasn't figured it all out either.

But they're figuring it out—together.

And that's the whole point, isn't it?

Love isn't about certainty. It's about trying. About showing up. About holding hands even when the world doesn't understand.

And somewhere, in every town, on every shore—

There are many Adams and Ishaans.

Boys who learn to name their hearts.

Who fight fear with truth.

Who choose love—despite everything.

And they are humans, too.

Their feelings are real.

Their love is valid.

And they deserve a world that celebrates them, not silences them.